THE COMPLETE WORKOUT

by Jordan Bailey

ISBN-13: 9781005262020
ISBN-10: 1477123456

Cover design by: Jordan Bailey
Library of Congress Control Number: 2018675309
Printed in the United States of America

CONTENTS

CHAPTER I: SHEMALE WORKOUT

I had just finished my routine when I heard the door to the gym open and close.

It was him. The young pool boy. He was wearing his staff issued black polo shirt and khaki cargo shorts, both of which looked like they were a size too small. He was carrying a short pool scrubber in one hand with a bag of wet leaves in the other, and so far, seemed unaware of my presence.

I was a regular at the gym, an amenity that came as a perk at the apartment complex. It had it all. Treadmills, weights, leg presses. Everything I needed to keep up my athletic figure.

I'm a fitness coach you see, but even in my spare time I was working out. I took pride in my work, standing a little over six feet tall with long, blonde hair and a full, ample 38 E bust. And I admit, relished in the looks and gazes from the men at the gym anytime I was out in public. But recently, I only cared about one - the pool boy. The very reason I began to frequent the complex's gym where he worked.

I sat up from the workout bench, slamming the barbell down on the rack above. The metal startled him and he jumped to attention, finally noticing me. I stood, grabbing my towel while pretending to just now see him too. It was a brief and subtle exchange, the way strangers may notice one another, but I gave a slight, calculated smile to start the game.

As I began to wipe myself off I looked myself over, noticing my damp attire and throbbing, muscular limbs. Thick globs of sweat gleamed and beaded off my massive, pulsating chest from my recent routine. My hair was in a ponytail but various strands of golden, wet locks dangled down over my face. When I turned back to him he was staring. I thought he was going to drop his tools when our eyes met.

"S-sorry... miss?" the young boy said.

"Becker. But you can call me Briana. And it's quite alright. I was just finishing up."

He pulled his jaw off the floor and continued moseying about. It was like he wasn't sure what he was doing, or at least forgot what he came in here for. It was rather cute.

I soaked in more of him, looking the boy up and down, noticing his features and curvy, intoxicating figure.

"I've seen you around," I said. "You must work here at the complex. What's your name?"

We only spoke briefly but he said his name was Jaime. He was nervous the entire time. Probably because he was speaking to a busty blonde who towered over him by at least a foot. He said that he cleaned the pools in the apartment complex but also helped around the gym and that he liked working out too. He looked athletic enough, but was rather frail and petite, especially next to me. He also did not share many of the masculine features like other boys his age, which I liked. Instead he had thin shoulders and wide hips more akin to a girl. He wasn't so handsome as he was cute if that makes any sense. He had a mop of blonde, sun-bleached hair on his head above sparkling green eyes, full, pink lips and a cute, girly button nose. He was much shorter than me, maybe 5'4", had only subtle muscle mass, and didn't appear to have any body hair. But the best part, my God, was his ass. Whether it was his tiny shorts or good genes, he had an ass that wouldn't quit. It was astonishing to see something so well fed, two perfectly round, fleshy globes wrapped in his golden, tanned skin.

There was just something about him, I thought as we chatted. It was his petite, almost feminine frame, his lithe musculature, and most definitely his wide, child bearing hips.

You see, I liked my boys just like Jaime. And so, ever since I spotted him a few weeks ago I was hooked. I knew I had to know more. I knew I had to corner him and coax or invoke some interest from him. Because almost every night since, when I would masturbate, it wasn't some muscle bound body builder type I was fantasizing about, it was Jaime and his luscious, round bubble butt.

So all that time had led to this. Our chance meeting alone in the gym. Little did he know how long I had watched him. I didn't think the boy ever noticed my stares. At least that's what I thought...

Thankfully, the boy spent most of his time eyeing my chest. Or at least trying not to. I certainly made it easy with my low cut sports bra. That was the point really, but I would have hated to scare him away if he may have noticed the swollen, baseball-sized bulge in my skin-tight fitness shorts.

I led the conversation, telling him about my work and my hobbies. He was enthralled but shy. It was cute. I told him about a client I had to work with over the weekend but suggested we both work out sometime. I told him I may be able to assist him if he was truly wanting to exercise more or bulk up.

He excitedly agreed but it was getting late. I certainly didn't want to get him into any trouble, and liked teasing my prey anyway, so I politely said my goodbyes and made my exit.

"Well you have a nice evening, Jaime. And a good weekend. I'll see you around." I said with a sly grin.

"Y-you too, Miss Becker. G'night."

I gave him a long look and left him to his devices. But I did catch him staring at my ass as I left the facility. At home I showered and readied for bed, expecting to have to leave early in the morning to drive across town. However, at just past 10 p.m. My client texted me to reschedule. Suddenly, I was free all weekend and I kicked myself for not pursuing young Jaime earlier.

It was Friday evening, and after confirming the reschedule, I decided to have a couple bottles of wine and watch a movie. So after dinner I retreated to my bedroom, glass in hand. I changed into something to sleep in, panties and an oversized t-shirt, then curled up in bed. Yet when the movie failed to keep my attention I procured my phone and began to browse.

Now, I don't generally look up or seek out pornography, but as I perused the various dating apps, the images of cocks and breasts began to take their toll.

My thoughts quickly returned to Jaime, the nudity on my phone fueling my mental images of his luscious, tanned body. Soon my panties grew tight. The growing inhabitant yearning to escape and be addressed. In tune with the film's sex scene, I slid my panties off, letting my smooth, engorging, eight inch cock spring forth and breathe. When I gripped it, my balls twitched and I began to slowly stroke my length up and down.

While I worked, I whispered to myself...

"Oh yeah, Jaime. You like that?"

I yanked my shirt up, cupping my left breast and squeezing my nipple. "Mmm, you like that big cock in your tight little boy hole, you little slut? Mmm, yeah Jaime! You're a nasty little slut, huh?"

I spread my legs out on my lush bedspread, envisioning the boy riding me. "Take my fucking cock, Jaime. Take that cock you little whore!"

My stroking got faster. I felt small trails of pre-cum leaking down my shaft and over my hand. The idea of fucking little Jaime had me over-enthralled. I tightened my grip, envisioning slipping into his virginal hole, trying to simulate the tight little ring stretching around my shaft. My little trick summoned more guttural moans, and I let loose a string of lewd vulgarities as I felt my orgasm rising.

Yet as I verbalized my fantasy, I suddenly caught movement in the mirror and saw a face looking through the crack in the door!

"What the?!" I blurted.

It was Jaime! And as soon as he knew he was caught, he bolted.

"Shit!" I thought to myself as I yanked my t-shirt down around me and ran out of the bedroom.

Frantically I moved, making sure it hung well past my knees to hide my genitals. As I reached the stairs, I could see Jaime fumbling with the front door.

"Stop! Hold it right there!" I shouted!

Jaime froze.

"What in the HELL do you think you're doing?" I continued, stomping down to the first floor.

He didn't answer. Instead he took a step backwards and turned around to face me. Like a student who had just gotten in trouble with his teacher.

After reaching the bottom of the stairs, I crossed my arms and glared at him. He shivered in place, dressed in the same work clothes. I looked at him, waiting for an answer while he wouldn't, or maybe couldn't, make eye contact with me.

"Well?! Why are you here? How did you even get in here?" I huffed.

"Well, um, I-I was just finishing my shift a-and..." He stammered, near-uncontrollably, never looking at me. "And I was walking by on my way home. And I saw all your lights were off so I thought you weren't here. So I'd, you know, so I used my key. I'm sorry, Miss Becker, I shouldn't have done that."

I took a step closer, "didn't think I was home? What were you planning on doing? Stealing from me?"

He shook his head, shrinking as I approached. "N-n-not exactly…"

"No? What then?"

"I… I like to watch you, Miss Becker…"

I watched as his face flushed red. I was a bit shocked at him just admitting it. I had caught him staring a few times around the complex but to actually hear him say it was something else entirely!

There was a moment of silent realization as we both sat there not knowing what to say. I wasn't sure who was more embarrassed, me or him. Although, as the seconds passed, I understood that I hadn't really done anything wrong. So it was time to have some fun with him.

"I know you look at me too," he blurted, testing a glance back at me. "I… I've seen you."

I sat there with my heart pounding for what felt like an eternity. "Jaime, I don't know what to say."

More silence followed before Jaime took a deep breath and said, "It's okay, Miss Becker. I look at you too."

The way he phrased it made me think. I cocked my head to one side, "look at me when?"

More silence as he turned away, "you know, like, in the gym and at the pool and stuff."

He still had barely looked at me, instead keeping his eyes on the floor. Though if he had, he may have seen my ever-hardening nipples through my shirt.

"Stuff?" I asked. "Like today? Jaime," I asked with a tone, "or have you watched me before?"

Jaime sat there for another moment before he replied, his voice cracking, "Yes, Miss Becker. I've done it before. I'm sorry! I know it's wrong. I shouldn't have done it. I shouldn't have done any of it-"

"Any of what?" I barked.

He almost burst into tears when I took another step forward, "what else have you done?"

His lower lip trembled, "I... I..."

"Out with it!" I said, feigning anger.

"Once..." he paused, fidgeting. "When you weren't home. I... I took a pair of your panties!"

He recoiled as if I was about to slap him.

I thought about it. Truly. But instead, I smirked. "Really? What for?"

It took him another moment to emerge from his shell. He looked at me briefly, then immediately diverted his eyes back to the floor.

"They smelt so good. Smelt like you. And... and I wanted to wear them," he sniffled.

This little slut, I thought, trying to supress my smile. A petite little androgynous boy with a fat ass who liked to wear panties? This boy might be the complete-fucking-package.

"Wearing girls' panties and sneaking around won't get you laid, Jaime." I kept up my glare, "what kind of girl do you think likes that sort of thing?"

He finally summoned the courage to look back at me, "I... I don't like the other girls."

I sat there for a moment, looking him over. God damn he was cute. With another step forward I was on him, then I reached down and lifted his tear stained face to look him right in the eyes.

"You're still a virgin, aren't you?"

He looked at me and nodded before more tears started.

"And you're wearing my panties right now, aren't you?"

He wiped his tear-streaked face then slowly nodded.

"Let me see."

Jaime's face went wide with shock, eyes nearly popping out of his skull and mouth agape in surprise.

"Go on. Turn around and show me. I wanna see your ass in my panties."

I think he knew the ruse was up. But he played along, probably because he wanted it. So slowly, he turned and, still sniffling, hooked his thumbs in his waistband and bent over, taking his shorts with him. What burst forth was a breathtaking sight - his succulent, bubbly ass. Two huge cheeks bulging from a tiny waist. I had only caught glimpses of it contained in shorts or jeans, but now before me was his perfect, heart shaped buttocks in one of my white thongs.

"Mmm," I hummed, licking my lips. "More. Bend over more."

And as he did I swiftly pulled my shirt over my head, unveiling my body to the room. He remained unaware though, instead facing forward still, no doubt beat red in embarrassment. Fully nude, my nipples stiffened at the touch of air. My lean, muscular body felt good out in the open. No matter how much he may have seen before, I knew little Jaime wasn't ready for the sight. He didn't notice at first. Too busy bending and peeling the shorts down his legs, but when he did finally glance back over a shoulder, he froze once more.

"Good boy," I said, my hands on my hips and my engorged cock heaving along with my breathing, growing harder by the second. When his shorts were off he turned, face flushed and thong tight against his nethers. He stood there a moment, staring at my dangling, but hardening meatstick. His thick ass stretched the limits of the thong, and its fabric hitched tighter from his small but turgid erection at his front.

Without another word, I found myself leaning forward and planting a small kiss on Jaime's supple, pink lips. He didn't pull away, so I kissed him harder and he kissed back, opening his mouth instead, so I pushed my tongue inside.

Holy shit this kid kissed like a pro and had my cock hard instantly. I couldn't believe this was happening. He was so eager! A pleasant surprise but a surprise nonetheless. After a minute I felt his hand moving up my leg to my crotch. He grabbed my throbbing dick and sent shivers through my body. I pulled off the kiss and looked at him. Gone was the scared boy of a few minutes ago. Instead was a cock hungry, little femboy slut.

"Are you sure you've never done anything before?" I chuckled.

He shook his head, "never." He replied. "But I've wanted this... for a long time."

Then he started kissing me again, fishing for my cock with his tiny digits. I knew I should have stopped him, but I wanted this apparently as much as he did. He wrapped his hand around my shaft and moaned into my mouth as he stroked it.

This time he pulled out of the kiss and looked at me. Then he smiled as he lowered to his knees until his lips met with the head of my spear. Instantly, his warm wet mouth was around my cock and I gasped. Jaime went to work as best he could but he could only get half of my fat monster in his mouth before he was gagging on it. But damn he was doing a fantastic job for a beginner! Internet porn had obviously taught him something.

I was so turned on that I grabbed the back of his head and started forcing him onto more of my hungry muscle. He gagged and sputtered as I forced more and more into his throat, but he never objected. I became possessed, put my other hand on his head, grabbing his hair. I used more and more force on the kid's head, pushing him further down on my rod. He kept gagging and choking as I raped his throat, but when I pulled out to let him breathe, he made no objections to his treatment.

This scene had me so close to cumming, I knew I wouldn't last. And when I forced Jaime down, I gave one final push and crammed my cock to the base. I held him tight as I felt him struggling for air, his throat muscles squeezing my dick, and that did it. My cock swelled even bigger and I shot into his throat.

"Oh, fuck!" I pulled out a bit and dumped the rest of my load into the little sluts mouth. Jaime swallowed what I gave him and kept sucking, getting every drop he could get into his hungry, depraved, little mouth.

When I had given him my last I let him unsheathe my cock from his throat. He gasped for air, breathing heavy with tears streaming down his face.

He yelped! It was beyond erotic. A high-pitched squeal as if I was tickling a young girl. I twirled my tongue around it, tasting every sweet flavor the boy released. Mere seconds later, to my surprise but in typical teenage fashion, he came.

With a buck and a groan, Jaime screamed, "Oh, God. Oh, fuck! I'm... I'm cumming Miss Becker!"

A second later my mouth was quickly filled with a big load of tasty boycum. It tasted like heaven. I concentrated on the sensitive head of his tiny prick while his body shook and convulsed. He squirmed as it happened, trying to free his hands and push my head off of him, but I held fast. I think it was an act. The way he futility jostled, seemingly unable to free his hands.

Yeah, he liked being shackled. He liked being my plaything.

"Please..." he begged. "I can't take any more!"

I pulled off and looked at him still shaking from the intense orgasm. Then I climbed on top of his quaking body and planted my mouth on his. As he responded to receive me, I opened my mouth, releasing the load of his cum that I had held.

He gulped it down, moaning as he was fed his own semen.

Holy fuck. This boy was a gold mine.

Retreating back down to his groin, I pushed his legs in the air, spreading his silky, white buttcheeks apart. There before me was the promised land. A perfect, hairless, pink boyhole, just waiting to be conquered. I leaned down, stuck out my tongue then flicked it against the tiny orifice and he moaned as my tongue ran over his hot little hole. I licked him a few more times, relishing the taste of his teenage ass before planting my mouth right on his pucker. Lips wrapped around it, I stuck my tongue in Jaime's tight little rectum. He jumped, nearly getting away from me, but I held him in place.

"Oh my God, Miss Becker. That's! That's soooo... good!" He cried out. "Mmm! F-fuck! I've never felt anything like it!" He purred, squirming.

I feasted on that luscious hole for ten minutes, pushing my tongue as deep as I could into that sweet young exit. Jaime just continued to moan and encourage me verbally. I relished in how loud and how eager he was! It turned me on beyond belief!

After I got his little boypussy nice and wet, I licked my middle finger and popped it inside him. Jaime's eyes flew open as a new, louder gasp escaped his mouth. He shuddered as I pushed more in, easily sliding to my knuckle. Once there I twisted and flicked, stretching it open. After just a few strokes I pulled it out and licked it, re-applying my saliva to his anus. When I crammed it back in, he let out a long, low moan, his greedy hole sucking on my finger.

I must have finger fucked him for another ten minutes, stretching him open more and more. My cock grew harder and harder with each passing second, oozing dribbles of pre-cum down onto the bed. I almost enjoyed teasing myself, knowing the longer I waited the sweeter the reward.

Finally, I could wait no longer. I pulled my fingers out and gripped my cock, smearing my pre-cum over its helmet. Jaime's eyes glowed with lust as he watched me sit up and lube up my fat length. I imagined what he saw, my heavy tits heaving from my deep breaths, my nipples hard as diamonds and my lips and chin a mess of saliva. I knew I looked like a sexy amazon goddess and now it was time to pillage.

So slowly, I inched forward, gently lifting his left leg up by the ankle and placing the aching head of my cock against his soon-to-be-destroyed hole. It was so warm and wet. I could feel his puckered lips trying to open and wrap around it. I licked his raised calf as I held him there...

"Ready to get fucked little virgin boy?"

He bit his lip and nodded.

"Good. It's gonna hurt," I warned him. "And I'm not going to stop no matter how much you beg or plead. Understand?"

"Y-yes, Miss Becker." He answered with a weak nod, uncertainty and fear tinged in his words.

With that, I pushed. Leaning into him. My pelvis moving unwavered. I could feel my head entering his pussy, the hole slowly opening to receive it. Jaime gasped, pinning his eyes closed and gritted his teeth, determined to take it just like he promised.

I grunted. I was determined. A bloodlust came over me as I entered the tightest, hottest asshole I had ever violated. All of it was going inside! I wasn't going to stop until my balls were rubbing against the little sluts' hairless hole.

Then the magic happened. My mushroom head popped through his anal ring and his hole squeezed behind it, locking it inside of him. Jaime clenched onto the sheets and screamed! His entire, lithe body trembled as I sunk more and more inside.

"Oh fuck, fuck, fuck!" Jaime cried out, breathing fast and shallow. It was if he was hyperventilating! But between his huffs of breaths he moaned, "Mmmmm. It's sooo fucking... BIG!"

I smiled. "Good little whore." I grunted again as I sank in with astonishing ease.

His cock twitched when I said the word. He loved it, I thought. And so did I. Yet for a few seconds, I paused, letting his hole get more adjusted to my girth. But as soon as his breathing slowed down I started pushing more of my womanhood into him.

JORDAN BAILEY

"Relax, baby! Let me in!" I ordered. He immediately complied with a slow, deep breath and my cock slid into him easier. "That's it. You're gonna take it all..."

"Oh, fuck!" He started howling as I continued my advance. Then, a few inches later, I felt my balls on his ass. I looked down. It was all inside!

"Oooooooooohhhhhhh," he cried as I bottomed out inside of him.

He had done it! I was balls deep in the boy. And damn was I impressed! I knew women who couldn't handle my cock, and here was this kid who took it near-effortlessly on the first, virgin try!

I leaned down and kissed him. He clutched my tits with either hand and kissed me back. Long and hard our tongues danced, and he licked my chin and lips as if to savor his own taste. My cock throbbed every few seconds, hot and ready to assault the boy.

"How's your first cock, little Jaime?" I asked.

"G-good..." he murmured, still shivering. "I've wanted this for so long. I've... wanted you for so long, Miss Becker..."

Then I felt his legs wrap around my lower back, and I knew he was ready.

"Oh, yeah?" I purred, flashing a wicked smile.

He nodded as I leaned back up, spreading his legs by the thighs. He looked intoxicating, the hairless, feminine boy with his blonde hair and tiny dick, spread out like a feast with a fat piece of girlmeat in his ass.

And then, I started, slowly pulling a little bit out, and pushing my cock back in. Jaime squeaked and squealed each time I thrusted. Little by little I increased the amount of meat I was sliding back and forth into the boy. He clung to the bed, moaning like a bitch in heat each time. Pretty soon I picked up my pace, fucking him with almost the whole length. In and out I moved, greedily pummeling to illicit more and more succulent, boyish screams.

Just when I thought he was going to break, when his breathing suffered and his eyes rolled back into his skull, when his body went limp and he looked as if he was about to pass out, I stopped.

It took him a moment to come to. He looked up at me, blinking.

Suddenly and swiftly I pulled out of his ass and he gasped as my fat head popped out of his hole. Before he could question me, I flipped him onto his stomach and spread his cheeks apart, admiring his now gaping boyhole.

"Life your butt up, slut." I said, guiding his backside to a suitable level. He arched his back, letting his plump ass protrude further.

"Good. Now tell me you want it, boy. Come on, tell me you want my big cock back in your little pussy!"

I rubbed then squeezed his right cheek before SLAPPING it hard.

"Ow! Y-yes! I want it, Miss Becker!" He said, breathing heavy. "I want it."

"What was that, slut? Speak up you little whore! Do you want me fucking your sweet little pussy or not?"

"Oh God, yes! I am a slutty little whore! Fuck me Miss Becker! Fuck me with your giant cock, please!"

I didn't even let him finish before I plunged my entire length back into the waiting depths of Jaime's (no longer) virgin hole.

"Aaaaaaahhhhhh!" He cried out as my balls slapped against his. Our new position allowed me greater access to his insides so

I grabbed his slim waist and started pounding his defenseless innards.

"Is this what you wanted, whore?" I huffed as I slammed against him harder and harder. "Is this what you wanted when you were spying on me, faggot? My big fat cock ripping your little pussy open?"

"Oh-oh G-god y-yes M-miss B-Becker!" He managed to sputter between my hard, pelvic thrusts. He began throwing his lower half at me each time I thrusted, fucking himself on my pole. "Fuck my faggot pussy! Fuck me harder!"

I grabbed Jaime's shoulders so I could pound his cunt even deeper and harder. Sweat gleamed off my body. My balls hit him with wet, heavy smacks. My tits bounced and thrashed about. I became an animal, grunting and howling, clawing and scraping at his once perfect, porcelain skin.

"That's right slut! I'll fuck this pussy whenever I want from now on! Anywhere I want. Day or night. Is that what you want bitch? My little high school bitch boy?"

"Y-yes... Miss-Miss Becker..." he huffed, cock drunk.

"And not just me. But anyone I want. All my friends are gonna get a taste! You hear me? You like girlcock? Then that's what you'll get! You're gonna be a little whore for me!"

"Oh God, yes! Please Miss Becker, make me your whore! I'll do whatever you want!"

"That's right slut! And we're gonna gangbang your faggot ass until you're full of cum." I shouted as I slid my fingers around his neck, pulling his head back, forcing him to arch his back more. My other hand gripped his now red ass, slapping hard and in unison every few times I thrusted.

Then I got up on my feet, hunching over him, allowing me a downward articulation into his guts. I paused just briefly in my new position so I could lean into his ear and whisper, "cause that's what you are faggot. You were born to get fucked and nothing else. That's why you have that pathetic little dick. You're nothing but two holes for me to use. That's what you were born for. That's all you are."

Jaime cried out as I degraded him. I could feel his boypussy squeeze my cock. Suddenly and violently, he screamed as his dicklet twitched, unloading volleys of cum onto the sheets below him. First just one spurt before stopping, then when I thrusted into him, another spray came forth, over and over until his miniscule balls were empty.

I could feel my own orgasm building as I rose in ferocity, punctuating each word with a hard slam as deep in him as I could get-

"PATHETIC... LITTLE... SLUTTY... FAGGOT... WHORE!"

With one final push, I buried my cock deep and I unleashed a deluge of semen into him, flooding his insides with hot girlcum for the first time in his life. The sensation was incredible, and I held onto his ass while both my balls emptied, pump after pump. His ass ate it all, hungrily and willingly accepting my thick, hot gift.

I finished and collapsed down onto him while my dick oozed its final few drops into the boy's receptive guts.

When I had the strength, I rolled, pulling my now soft cock out of his wet hole. Jaime laid still, occasionally twitching and shuddering from his life changing orgasm. Wiping the sweat off my brow, I rolled him over until our eyes met. He had tears running down either cheek and his face was flushed red.

Smirking, I wiped the sweaty hair off his forehead and glared down at him.

For a second I felt guilt, remembering the horrible, but true, things I just barked at him. "I'm sorry." I started to say, "I kind of got carried away there."

But he silenced me with a finger to my lips. "Don't be sorry." He whispered. "It was perfect. You're perfect, Miss Becker."

I smiled and giggled, "Briana. My name's Briana."

"I know. But I like Miss Becker better," he said with a warm smile. "Oh, and I forgot to mention," he continued, blushing. "My mom is out of town and I'm off work. I can stay all weekend."

I looked deep into his sparkling green eyes, kissed him, then whispered, "you little slut."

THE END (of Part One)

CHAPTER II: SISSY WORKOUT

The rest of the weekend was like living a dream. I fucked my new little slut so many times I could hardly believe he was able to walk on Monday. We had sex in every room of my apartment and in every position imaginable. Little Jaime was a gift from the Gods. He was heavenly. A petite yet voluptuous blonde that I just could not get enough of. He was obedient and cock hungry throughout our weekend together. He blew me when I wanted, he licked me where I wanted and he let me put myself where I wanted. What's more, he loved every second of it. Jaime was submissive naturally it seemed, and followed any command I gave without question. He was perfect, I thought, at least so far...

In mere hours of our first encounter he had mastered deep throating. All eight inches of my girldick. After that he was taking my cock in his ass dry without any hesitation. He drank my semen without question, no matter where I came, sometimes even licking it off the bed or the floor.

By Saturday he had already found my weak spots so he could service my body like a professional. A playful lick or pinch of a nipple, a stern grip on my breast when I fucked him too hard, or suckling on one or both of my smooth balls when he went down on me. Whatever I wanted, consciously or not. He was the perfect specimen for my carnal desires.

On Sunday Jaime's mother returned home and found him missing. But when she called to check in, I was balls deep in the boy. There was no time to stop. Not then. It would take much more than that to stop me, no matter how much he pleaded. And so while he phoned her back I kept up my fucking, insisting he stay one more night with me. As they spoke, he was ass in the air, face down in pillows with my cock buried inside him, and I fucked him constantly. I was impressed that he was able to keep his composure as I mercilessly pulverized from behind, feverishly trying to convince his mother he was staying the night with a friend. She agreed without issue, and when he hung up, I grabbed my little Jaime by the hips, pulled him in and viciously finished, rewarding his sweet boypussy with another hot load of cum.

The next couple of weeks were fantastic. We were fucking on a daily basis. Sometimes it was after work, sometimes before, sometimes even during. Whenever he could sneak away from his duties at the pool or the gym. And whenever I felt like being serviced, Jaime was there to accommodate. It was easy for him to sneak out of his apartment and down the street to mine. And when he spent the night, I would use him as I saw fit, sometimes for hours on end. I could only imagine what my neighbors thought, hearing his girlish cries at all hours of the evening...

My latest form of degradation started just a few days ago - video.

On a whim one night I pulled my phone while he was sucking my dick. We had just been watching TV when he felt my hard-on and went to work. In mid fellatio I watched him through the phone's screen, eagerly sucking the head and licking up and down the shaft. Before long I came all over his face, capturing the moment and the aftermath as he licked up his mess. His only plea, he said after, was that I 'please don't show anyone.'

I told him I would do whatever I wanted with it. What, I had no idea, but I wasn't about to let him dictate my actions. He blushed when I shot him down and asserted myself. I couldn't help but think he liked that too.

More pictures and videos followed. I liked to look at them while we were apart. I would watch them on my way to work, standing in line at the store, in between workout sessions with clients, or just if I was bored. They were hotter than any porn I had ever seen.

Before long, people around me began to notice my mood, quoted as more upbeat and relaxed. Now, I was cheerful and happy to begin with, but lately I positively glowed with radiance. Even I could tell the change when I looked at myself in the mirror. But no matter who pried, I just smiled and laughed, shook my head or shrugged. I wasn't ready to tell anyone the gem I had discovered. More importantly, I don't think Jaime's true self was ready to be unveiled to the world.

But one day as the spa was closing, my close friend and co-worker, Erin, finally came into my office with a look in her eye.

"So who are they?" she asked, closing the door behind her.

Erin was stunning. A roughly six foot, buxom brunette with medium-length brown hair and a blinding smile. She was the masseuse at the spa we both worked at, and was just as in-shape as I, with a hefty chest and curvy, athletic figure.

"I don't know what you mean." I lied, trying to remain preoccupied with wrapping up for the day.

"Come on Bree, don't lie. I know you too well." She slinked forward. "You wouldn't be this chill if you weren't getting some."

She smiled, seeing right through me. She did know me. We had worked together for years and been friends for longer. But at first I doubted how well she truly could define.

When I didn't answer, she continued, "I can see it written all over you. So c'mon you minx, who is it? Boy or girl? Or..."

I rolled my eyes as she reached my desk. One couldn't help but stare at her chest. Her tits were massive and may very well have been bigger than mine. They were two huge, plastic orbs restrained behind a tight sports bra. Like nearly every other day, she wore a matching, skin tight set of all white workout clothes.

23

Erin just looked back and kept smiling, eventually sitting on the corner of my desk.

I shook my head, "nope! I'm not telling!"

I wasn't afraid to tell her because of Jaime's age or gender. After all, we were both into the same 'type' of guy. I was afraid because I knew she would want a piece of him. She always did. A chance to steal them away, or worse. Nearly all my trans friends fought over boys and girls alike and a majority of my friends were real, perverted sluts. Especially the likes of Erin, April, Mia and Veronica... especially Veronica.

"Oh, no!" Erin huffed. "You're not getting off that easy. I'm not leaving this office until you tell me."

I shut down when she changed tone. I wasn't about to respond if she was going to be a bitch about it. But then she changed her strategy.

"Aw. C'mon, Bree. I won't tell anyone. I promise! Please?" Erin said, clasping her hands together to emphasize her begging.

I rolled my eyes again. She was like a child. But a child in manners and that was all. After looking into her giant, brown, puppy dog eyes for a moment, I shirked and relented.

"Okay! Fine! I admit *they* exist. We just met a few weeks ago. Now will you leave me alone?"

"What? No way! Now you gotta tell me more! Come on Bree, we have no secrets, right? Boy or girl?! C'mon!"

This bitch.

Although, I must admit, it was exciting just thinking about Jaime. I wanted to gush about him. I wanted to smother her with details.

But I had to show at least some restraint, right?

I shook my head and rolled my eyes again. I guess I did secretly want her to know. There was no way I was going to let her 'steal' Jaime away. Not like she even could. Well, maybe she could. But forget about that.

Because suddenly the idea sparked a new interest. I had never been with more than one partner before. Never a threesome or anything. But the idea of two giant girlcocks violating Jaime was enticing. I had seen Erin naked. And her me. We were practically best friends but never been romantically involved. What if I did share? It was no secret we all liked the same type, more or less.

Finally, I answered, "Boy." I said coily, knowing it would pique her interest. "Do you even have to ask?"

She lit up like a Christmas Tree, "Are you kidding? I would've been surprised if not."

We both giggled and my gears began to turn. I wondered if she would be interested in a threesome as well. I looked her over again, trying to read her body language. The idea was growing on me.

"Aaand? Is he cute?" She asked.

I just laughed, "Oh yeah. Cute as a button. A little girly but in a good way."

"Yeah? Well come on, I want all the details! Blonde? Brunette? Young? Big dick? C'mon, out with it!"

"Blonde hair. Well, more dirty blonde I guess. And young would be the truth. Although a bit of an understatement. "

She leaned on my desk and looked me in the eyes. "No way!" She blurted loudly.

I looked back and smiled, licking my teeth. "Way."

"Aaand! C'mon Bree, stop teasing me!" She jostled in place like a spoiled brat in a toy store. Her breasts jiggled and she pinched her groin.

Holy shit. She was getting excited.

"Jeez Erin, you're a bigger slut than he is. Okay, okay. His name's Jaime. And I would barely call whatever he has a 'dick'. But that's not important. He makes up for it in the ass department."

She didn't respond at first. Instead eagerly awaited more details, her eyes sparkling with excitement. "Wow. Okay, I'm totally jealous. Where'd you meet him?"

"He works at the apartment complex. At the pool."

She giggled, "a little pool boy? You naughty girl! So? What else? Wait, is THAT what you've been doing these past weekends?"

"Oh, yeah. Literally all weekend!"

"You little minx!"

"And..." I said, looking her right in the eyes. "The little slut does anything I want."

I let that shocking revelation sink in for a moment. I swear I could see Erin's cock twitch in her yoga pants.

"H-how old is he?" She managed to ask.

"Just turned eighteen" I whispered.

"Holy fuck." She said, almost gasping.

"Sounds like you struck gold! Does he have a brother?" Erin asked, laughing. That's when I knew she was hooked too. Sure enough. I had found another cock for my hungry little whore. And I didn't even know I was looking.

"Here," I said. I moved around my desk and pulled my phone out. I had to skim through for a bit, but soon enough I found the correct photo I held it up for Erin to see: It was a beautiful shot of Jaime's freshly fucked hole, gaping open, cum dripping out of it and down his tiny balls.

"Oh my God! You nasty bitch!" She said, grinning and pinching her crotch again.

I scrolled to another pic, this one with Jaime on his back with his hands holding his legs up, proudly displaying his shame. Below his tiny dicklet was mine, fat and swollen, half in his ass. Erin licked her lips. I noticed her nipples getting hard and poking through the thin fabric of her top. I scrolled to a video next. This one showing my big cock sliding in and out of Jaime's sweet hole as I fucked him from behind. With a tap on the screen, it started playing, audio and all...

"What do you want, faggot?" my voice filtered through.

"Please Miss Becker..."

I had paused, pulling my cock out of him while I recorded.

"What do you want, you whore? Say it! Look back at the camera and tell me, bitch." Jaime turned and looked straight into the lens, his eyes pleading.

"I'm a slut. I'm a whore. I only exist to serve you. Please put your cock back in my pussy! Please fill me full with your cum!"

"Thatta girl," I purred, sliding my veined womanhood all the way back into the hilt.

Jaime moaned until the video stopped and began to automatically replay.

Erin just stood there wide-eyed and awestruck with her mouth open. I looked down, spotting her raging erection trying to escape her pants. It was so fucking hot. Just like the rest of her. Her cock was bigger than I remembered. Though I don't recall ever seeing it hard.

"So..." I began, "do you wanna come over some time?"

I bit my lip and looked back at Erin, who was still glued to the screen.

"We can put some panties on it," I started, feeling my cock twitching when I called Jaime 'it'. He truly was a thing. A thing to be used. And by the looks of her body reacting, Erin totally agreed.

"Maybe a bra? A little make up? And its dick is so tiny you won't even notice it. I think his bright red lips would look sooo good sucking on your cock, Erin."

I knew I had her.

Erin, like our mutual friend Veronica, had a thing for sissies and crossdressing. It wasn't something I necessarily needed or wanted, after all I had been perfectly content with fucking him non-stop for weeks. But I had to admit it to myself as I broached the subject, the idea of dressing Jaime up did excite me.

After a beat and a blink of realization, Erin finally looked back at me. "When?"

I thought for a moment, "Friday. I'm going to have him stay all weekend again."

"Pink." Was all she said next, breathing heavy. Her massive bulge and erect nipples literally jutted from her clothes. "Pink bra and panties."

A smile crept across my lips. Just thinking about Jaime in all manners of lingerie I could force him into nearby drove me wild on the spot.

"You got it." I said, winking. "But you uh, might wanna do something about that though," I smiled, pointing to her groin and blushing along with her.

We laughed it off and readied to leave. It was six o'clock and all the clients were gone. A few minutes later and we had said our goodbyes in the parking lot. All of a sudden my weekend was booked and it had turned into something far more tantalizing than I could have imagined. Jaime, Erin and I. Holy shit. I couldn't wait...

When I got home that evening, Jaime was already inside. He was in the kitchen, eating cereal, clad in his same black polo and tiny, khaki bottoms. His ass looked so good hanging out of those shorts, I couldn't help myself. I was so pumped full of adrenaline thinking about Friday night and getting to share my slutty little blonde boy. Without saying a word I pounced on him. He gasped and squealed, feigning resistance. I ripped his shorts off, slammed him down on the counter and jammed my cock inside his warm depths.

He screamed. I loved it.

Fucking Hell. Even though I had been violating him almost daily, he was still incredibly tight. I had also, up until now, usually loosened him up first, but not tonight. Not with the thoughts of spit roasting him with Erin, trading holes on a whim, fucking him mercilessly and violently because we could.

I grabbed Jaime's hair, forcing his face into the tile. I was fueled with an all new type of bloodlust, reveling in the fact that the boy had no idea what was soon going to happen to him.

Face down and ass up, I hammered Jaime from behind. He howled in pain but I didn't stop. I couldn't. And with each new thrust I sunk my huge cock more and more inside. I held his head with one hand, smashing his cheek against the countertop, and with my other hand I pulled his butt apart, watching my entire meat eventually, and repeatedly, disappear inside. I plowed his poor hole as hard as I could while he whimpered and cried beneath me. I showed him no mercy, even when he begged me to slow down. His tears and pleas only made me fuck him harder. By the time my climax approached, sweat was dripping off of me as I fucked my slut like an animal.

Despite his cries and screams of pain, my whore bucked and shuddered, then came on the side of the kitchen island, his hard little twitching phallus spasming as it unloaded. His orgasm made him clamp down on my cock. The sensation was unreal. Further astounding was him cumming without him or I even touching his little dicklet. He truly was becoming a woman.

His guts constricting me, I could hold out no more. I let out a primal howl as his cunt spasmed around my cock. Gripping him tight, I pumped his ravaged hole full. Pulse after pulse my balls emptied inside him. When I was finished I took a step back, letting my cock slide out and watching the pints of cum fall out of his anus.

Jaime laid motionless on the tabletop, aside from the occasional twitch, and when I checked on him I found out why – he had passed out!

I pinched his ass, assuming that would wake him. But to no avail. So instead I planted a kiss on his reddened cheek and whispered, "good girl, Jaime. Good girl. But you better clean that up, bitch."

I left him there, bottomless and bent over my counter, to go wash up. When I returned, having showered and changed, he was wiping up his mess like a good little girl. We ate dinner, watched a movie, and the rest of the night was filled with more visceral sex.

The next morning was more of our same routine. He woke me up with his lips on my cockhead. It wasn't so much as a blowjob as I used his face and lips to pleasure myself. I was rough like the night before. I wanted to fit all of my girth down his throat. I had to train his holes for Friday. Even when he gagged and his eyes went white, I held him tight as he struggled. Then I exploded in Jaime's throat. He choked and fought for air, trying not to drown. I chuckled, imagining how none of this would even compare to his coming double-team. Finally I let Jaime up for air, and he coughed and gasped, spitting up cum.

"Don't waste my cum you little whore." I said, guiding him back down. He hungrily went back down on me. "That's it... good girl."

Still barely conscious and struggling for air, he went to work cleaning, licking up what he spit out. When the mess was done he cleaned off my shaft, then my belly. What an amazing little slut...

Then we showered together, where I fucked him again. After that we would normally eat breakfast or just lounge around until he had to go to work. But this morning I ushered him to the front door right after our showering ritual. Barely dressed, I took him to the front door and nudged him outside.

"M-miss Becker, what's going on? Have I done something wrong?"

I looked at him coldly and said, "No Jaime. But I won't see you again until Friday night."

I had thought about it for some time. All night in fact. But assured myself this would be best. A few days without his holes and I would be wired by Friday. And so would he. I also wanted him extra horny. I wanted him to want it as much as I did. I wanted him to be begging for it by the time he saw me again. Plus I wanted his pussy to be as tight as humanly possible.

"Friday?" He asked. He looked as if he'd been hit in the gut.

"That's... that's four days. Why? I dunno if I can go without you that long."

"Well you better," I said as I kissed him. "But don't jerk off or play with your ass before then either. I have something special planned for you. Now do as you're told."

He reached for his shorts and I snatched them out of his hands. "I'm keeping these. Now get your sweet ass home and I'll see you Friday."

He looked at me with a little fear in eyes, "but... but someone might see."

"So what?" I said. I wasn't that worried. It was still early and barely anyone was out yet. And even then there was a layer of misty fog still hovering in the air. He'd make it home just fine. "Now. Do. As. You're. Told."

Jaime shrank, accepting defeat. And after a quick glance up and down the street, he scampered off bottomless. I smiled after him, watching his creamy white ass bounce down the street. A few seconds later he had vanished and I went inside, already dreaming about Friday.

The week was a busy one. I crammed all the appointments I could to free up my schedule over the weekend. Days that weren't spent visiting clients were spent at the spa, where Erin and I commiserated. Femininity Max Day Spa and Wellness Center housed all manner of luxury for both exercise and beauty treatment. Uniquely though, it was staffed almost entirely by trans women. Erin and myself were just two of many. But we also had the occasional man or woman employee, though I doubt they ever knew.

That Thursday at the spa, Erin crept back into my workout room after all my clients had left and shut the door behind her. I was gathering my things and didn't see her right away.

"Hey, Erin. Bout ready to head out?" I said. She was stunning as always, clad in tight yoga pants and sports bra like before.

"So, uh, Bree," she started, "about Friday…"

What now? I thought. "Don't tell me-" I started before she cut me off.

"I, uh, may have mentioned our little get together to-" She bit a nail and feigned a bashful look.

No. Fucking. Way. This bitch… What had she done now?!

"You what!? Erin, what the hell! You said you wouldn't tell anyone-"

She stepped closer inside, clasping her hands like before, "I know, I know. I'm sorry. It's just… I had to, okay? I mean, How could I not? After what you showed me! That video!?"

I slumped, begrudgingly picking up my floor mats and tidying up like normal. Perhaps I was to blame. Maybe I laid on the seduction too thick and led her on. I should have known. Erin had the integrity of a high school gossip queen.

I felt her eyes on me. Waiting on me. I held off as long as I could, wanting her to feel my spurn.

Finally, when my things were together, I looked at her and asked, "who'd you tell?"

She batted her eyelashes, looked me over with a fake 'innocent' smile and whispered, "Veronica."

Veronica Petracova. Probably the most beautiful 'women' I had ever seen or met. She was a stunning specimen, even by my standards, with a massive, ample chest, a terrific figure and full, luscious lips. She had dark features, like Erin, but was exotic in ways sailors told stories about. Some sort of Czech or Russian beauty created from absolute perfect genes.

She was a regular at the spa, and an occasional client. Although she in no way needed my athletic services, she had befriended most of the staff here, myself included. Aside from Erin, she was probably my next closest friend. Her and I just didn't work together so we didn't see each other as often. I may have had to keep up my ruse of frustration with Erin, but I secretly imagined what Veronica looked like naked, and even more wondered what she could offer our... 'party'.

"Do I even wanna know how this came up?" I asked.

"She was here the other day with a boy toy of her own and I... may have mentioned it. I'm sorry, okay. Really. But I just thought that-"

"Thought what?" I crossed my arms and glared.

"Thought it would be sooooo fucking hot," Erin giggled.

My mind wandered. Erotic images danced within. She was right.

I just looked at Erin for a moment, silently judging her. She was all smiles back, like she always was. Innocent yet devilish all at once. Finally, I said, "Okay, you tramp. Fine. But you bring the wine. And you owe me!"

Erin did a little first pump, "Yesss!"

"Tell no one else, okay? And neither one of you better mess this up, understand?!" I was trying to sound tough, but the thought of another 'girl' joining us made my cock stir. Especially one like Veronica.

"You have my word," Erin beamed. "I promise."

"Alrighty. Be at my house by eight."

And with that, Erin spun and skipped down the hall.

With a wiggle in my step and a smile on my face, I left work and went to the local mall. It was odd but arousing shopping for Jaime. A boy yet a girl. I wanted him to look his best, especially now that we had another new someone joining us. I wanted to make absolutely sure my little slut did not disappoint them.

I hit Necktoria's Secret first and picked out the perfect lingerie for him in no time. Crotchless panties, bra, stockings, a choker, garter belt, and see-thru mesh stockings. All in pink. Thanks to the tags on his shorts, I knew everything would fit. I even picked up a few sexy extra things for myself, so if little Jaime performed well, I may have a special something for him.

After that, I swung by the shoe store for a pair of pink stilettos. They were adorably sexy, with long straps that would tie and wrap around one's calves. I hoped Jaime would like them but at the same time didn't care. I liked them so he damn well better.

Everything accounted for, I headed home just before sunset.

When I pulled into the complex I saw a familiar sight, Jaime in the gym. It didn't look like he was working either. He was wearing some sort of tight, black workout gear that hugged his lithe, feminine body. I wanted a closer look. So parking swiftly, I took advantage of still being in my yoga outfit to strut into the gym and call out to him.

"Oh hey, Jaime was it?" I chirped, grabbing everyone's attention. Jaime's face went white. There must have been a dozen other patrons, mostly men, who were now all staring at us.

"Y-yes. M-miss Becker..." Jaime stuttered, absolutely terrified. I didn't care. I wanted to put my hands on him.

I kept up my ruse, "great to see you again. Did you still want some tips and help with a workout?"

"Um-"

"Oh, of course you do! Here, let me have a look at you."

I crept over him, straddling him as he laid on the bench press. As if we were totally platonic, I 'aided' him in his weight lifting form, guiding his arms up and down as he lifted the tiny barbell. It was amusing. There was barely any weight on it. I giggled as he strained with the most basic and petty movements but relished in his trembles of embarrassment as I 'coached' his process. His ass looked fucking incredible in his cute little shorts. I couldn't keep my hands off it, squeezing or kneading it when the opportunity presented itself. To torture him further, I would occasionally rub or caress an arm or a leg, sending shivers through his body.

This went on for hours. I put that boy through his paces that night at the gym. I made him do reps till his young body couldn't take anymore. I wanted him to be weak tomorrow. I wanted him to be sore inside and out. Throughout the workout I groped him, squeezing here, rubbing there. I'd casually lean into Jaime's ear and whisper so no one else could hear. I'd say things things like "good job faggot" or "keep up the good work slut." But my favorite moment was when I was helping him with his squats, a weightless barbell on his shoulders and his spandex shorts damp with pre-cum. I stood behind him as he squatted, letting my bulge rub against him each time he rose or lowered. God damn he was soft.

By the end of it all EVERYONE was looking. I wasn't making it subtle. I wanted everyone to see this young blonde boy rubbing his ass against me.

"You like all these men looking at you? Hmm? You fuckin' whore,"

I said to him softly.

He tried to ignore me, but I could tell it flustered him. Up and down he went, my throbbing bulge rubbing between his ass. His own hard little dick strained his shorts. There was no way to hide it. It was a glorious sight. He was blushing a bright red and I laughed at him, taunting the miniscule weight he was lifting. I had never realized how much I enjoyed fucking with someone like this.

Eventually, when most of the ogling patrons left, I told him we were done. When no one was looking I kissed him on the cheek, then pinched his ass. "Get some rest tonight, bitch. Big day tomorrow."

He shivered. In fact he may have come right then and there.

But enough was enough. And so with a wave and a smile, I headed for the door. It took every ounce of strength not to drag him out with me by an ankle. But I resisted temptation, knowing the wait will be all the more sweeter. Turning just as I was exiting, I called out-

"See you tomorrow little Jaime!"

The End (of Part Two)

CHAPTER III: TRIPLE WORKOUT

Friday seemed to drag on forever.

Erin had taken the day off so it was especially long with no one to talk to or pass the time with. But hours passed, and as a present to myself I left work early in preparation for the night.

After getting home and showering, I texted Jaime to come over and went to work compiling his new outfit. All the pieces were in place. But we only had a few hours to prepare for Erin and Veronica.

A few minutes later there was a knock on my door. It was Jaime, clad in his standard boyish but revealing attire. "Why hello there," I said with a smirk.

He didn't respond at first, barely able to even look at me. He had his arms behind his back and eyes on the ground, teetering on the balls of his feet.

I looked him up and down again, noticing his flushed cheeks and sheepish look, then cleared my throat to goad an answer.

Eventually, Jaime looked at me with a little panic in his eyes and meekly said, "H-hey M-Miss Becker..."

"Hey yourself. Ready for tonight?"

"I, um... I guesso," he said with a stutter. He was so cute, and he still had no idea what I had in store for him. "What's so special about tonight?"

"You'll see. Come in," I said, watching him as he entered. He rubbed his arms as he moved, as if chilled. "Go on upstairs. We need to get you ready."

Once inside, he turned and looked up at me with his big, puppy dog eyes. "Get me ready?"

I shut the door behind him then put my hands on my hips, "Yes. I have some friends coming over. And you're going to meet them."

Jaime stood there a moment just staring back at me. A very real fear tinged his face.

I stared back, unphased. "Didn't you hear me? Upstairs. Now!"

Whether from my command or from fear, he spun and scurried up the stairs.

When he was out of sight I glanced at my phone, checking the time. It was already seven o'clock and sure enough, I had already received texts from both Erin and Veronica. They were already on their way.

Jaime was waiting for me upstairs, sitting on the edge of the bed with his hands and legs crossed. He perked up as I entered but then I motioned him towards my bathroom. I placed him in front of the mirror and looked him over - he certainly was girly enough already, but how could I amplify it?

By now you've heard me gush over young Jaime's looks enough. I could talk about him and his scrumptious body for hours. But now, gazing down at his sheepish and delicate physique, I was ready to turn him into a woman. I noticed his normally shaggy blonde hair was more trimmed and pampered than normal, and wondered if he'd been taking the steps himself. His skin looked softer, and his succulent lips and massive eyes oozed pure sex even more than before. Had he been transforming on his own? And dare I say for me?

"Miss Becker, what are you-"

"Sshh," I cut him off. I had been staring and he caught me, "let's get you ready for your big debut."

"Big... debut?" He whispered in a hushed, inquisitive tone.

"Yes, Jaime. I told my friends they were meeting my new girlfriend tonight. So we'll have to do a little preparation to convince them."

He swallowed hard, looking nervous.

"You're pretty girly as it is though. So I don't think I'll have to do much."

I took out my makeup, matching his foundation and testing the various pigments of blush and mascara for the best fit, and went to work. I lined his eyes with thick, black eyeliner, topped it with globs of eye shadow, and darkened his thick lashes with crimson mascara. After that, I put a little blush on the cheeks, and used a sexy 'come-fuck-me' pink lipstick.

For the most part he was quiet throughout, silent and obedient. Though I think he secretly liked the feeling. The feeling of being turned into a woman. All-in-all the process was easy. I only needed to pluck a few hairs on his eyebrows and put a bit of product in his hair to make him completely passable. God I wished I had his genetics when I was younger...

After checking his already smooth arms and legs I started on his fingers and toes, slowly going over the teeny digits one by one for imperfections. Work was minimal, but his boyish fingernails wouldn't do. So I began the process of an impromptu manicure. I chose a sparkling, glittery pink for his refurbished nails to match the rest of his lingerie.

As I finished painting he finally spoke, "Miss Becker?" Jaime said, his eyes glued to the transformation happening before his very eyes. When I stopped to look at him he was staring back at his reflection, eyes wide with wonder.

Slowly and purposefully, I answered only after I had sealed the cap on the paint. "Yes?"

"Why did you tell your friends I was a girl?"

"First!" I huffed, grabbing his chin and putting my face to his.

"Don't ever question me."

A burst of fear flashed across his face.

"And second, what are you afraid of? Isn't that what you are?" I asked as I inspected the boy's nails one last time. "Worried my friends might find out you're a sissy, little bitch boy? And not some slutty girl?"

"I-" he upstarted but I silenced him with another jerk to his chin.

"What you think doesn't matter. What matters is you are to entertain them tonight. Do you understand?"

His look was priceless. Shear terror on his soft, pretty face.

"Jaime? Tell me you understand," I commanded.

Then slowly, he nodded. Nodded as best he could with my firm grip on his chin.

"Good. Now let's finish up. They'll be here soon."

Despite his worried or even terrified look, I could see his tiny little dick getting hard through his shorts. Whatever excuses he was trying to muster couldn't hide what his body truly wanted. My beautiful little slut.

After a final look over, I stood Jaime up and nudged him out into the bedroom. It was time to unveil his new attire. And just as I expected, as he stepped from the bathroom, little Jaime froze at the sight of the skimpy clothes laid out on the bed.

The lingerie was just like Erin had requested, a set of pink bra and thong panties. They were mesh-type garments, with solid pieces of fabric only where nipples or genitalia might be. I paired them with matching see-thru pink stockings, garter belt, choker and headband. The five inch heels completed the look, with long criss-cross straps that would run up the calf when worn.

"Are you... going to make me wear that?" Jaime asked, shocked. His face turned red, hidden partially by the newly applied makeup.

Legitimately frustrated at this point and pressed for time, I grabbed his wrist. "What did I JUST say?!" I growled, yanking him over to the clothes. "Now get dressed. And stop with the questions!"

He sat there and looked at the spread for a moment. Whether it was awe or excitement or fear I did not know. But slowly at first, he peeled off his boy clothes, getting nude before picking up the first sheer article. I watched, mouth salivating, as his supple body became nude then dressed itself in his new lingerie. I smiled, pleased how everything fit him. He hobbled in the heels, but he would get used to them.

When he was finished I moved behind him, whispering in his ear, "all done, little Jaime."

After a kiss on his neck I smelled him, wanting nothing more than to tear his clothes off and take him right then and there. But instead I shuffled him to my full-length mirror.

An audible gasp escaped his lips when his reflection came into view. With his curly blonde hair, pink painted lips, slutty attire and makeup, he really did look like a girl.

"What do you think?" I said, smiling back at our reflection from behind him.

He was in shock. Wide-eyed and in awe of his appearance.

"I-I'm a girl...." he murmured, realizing.

My smile grew wider, "You sure are."

He anxiously looked himself over, turning slightly either way to look at his sides and butt. His figure was immaculate, filling out the sultry lingerie in every way except his lack of breasts. I was just as enamored as he, but finally he smiled, blushing at himself.

But now it was time for business. Seriousness returning, I cleared my throat and said, "My friends will be here any minute. Go on and sit on the bed."

He complied, looking worried and scared again. "Miss Becker?"

I turned, waiting for his question that I was allowing.

"Are your friends..." he began sheepishly, "are your friends like you?"

So that's what he wanted to know. The little slut.

I smiled down at him as I headed for the door. "Cross your legs," I told him. He did, and that made the look complete. Sitting on my bed was a prim and petite blonde girl clad in pink stockings and lingerie.

My phone vibrated. It was my alarm for seven-thirty.

"Stay put until I call you," I ordered, closing the bedroom door. He nodded with a worried smile and I headed downstairs.

On my way I grabbed a trio of wine glasses from the kitchen and set them out. I had decided on spending the evening in the dining room. It was small, dimly lit with enough chairs and equipped with small end tables for our drinks. After double checking the arrangements I procured a bottle of bourbon that I knew Veronica liked, then lit a handful of candles next, making sure the lighting was perfect.

A few minutes later, the doorbell rang.

I was very pleasantly surprised when I answered the door. There they stood. My two guests, Erin and Veronica, were two dark-haired busty vixens ready and waiting for the surprise I had in store for them. Erin was a stunner as always, dressed in jean shorts and a skimpy, white tank top. Her cleavage was on full display, as it should be, and she wore tall boots that hugged her knees.

Veronica was right behind her, and literally took my breath away.

She was a six foot slice of villainous beauty, with a hefty, ample chest, long luscious legs and dark, wavy hair. Her outfit was even more revealing than Erin's, a black tube top and shredded jeans. I couldn't help but notice the way her flesh bulged out of the tears in her clothing, both top and bottom.

"Hey!" Erin called out as I opened the door.

"Hey guys, come on in." I said as we all exchanged hugs. "Holy cow, you two look great!"

I welcomed them into my home, holding the door for both of the dark haired amazons. They strode in like they owned the place, looking around presumably for their entertainment. I was astounded at Veronica's confidence, amicably strutting around, her eyes moving over my furniture, decor and wall art. She had no shame. The world was hers. She was the embodiment of prowess. Everything about her secreted pure, sexual energy. I couldn't wait for her to see Jaime. I couldn't wait to see her out of her clothes. She was a chiseled statue of sex. The perfect 'woman'. As she mused about I could see that her ripped pants bulged from a fat, softball sized package at her front and her breasts literally oozed out from her top.

Despite my thirst, we chatted a bit. Recanting how just a few days prior Veronica had brought her newest 'boytoy' into the spa. I think Bobbi was his name, a cute and feminine boy with an ass that rivaled little Jaime's. So as you could imagine Erin and I had all manner of intricate questions for Veronica and her newly acquired 'project'.

After the pleasantries I directed my guests to the dining room. I poured Erin and I wine and Veronica her whiskey, nestling between them as we each found our separate seats. When we were each settled in I popped my eyebrows and asked if they were ready. The pair smiled excitedly and nodded. Finally, it was time to start the festivities.

Standing, I checked myself in a nearby mirror. I wasn't sure which one of us looked best. But with a giddy Erin to my right and a smirking, sultry Veronica to my left, I cupped my hands around my mouth and called out to the scantily dressed boy upstairs...

"All right, slut. We're ready for you!" I called. There was a brief silence, then I heard the light footfalls down the staircase.

Hearing him get close, I stood by the staircase banister. A few seconds later and Jaime appeared at the top of the steps, looking every bit the girl he was playing. He held onto the rail and watched his feet so he wouldn't fall. There was a collective gasp from the girls' lips as the boy descended. When he reached the bottom he looked around, then froze at the sight of the two beautiful brunette 'women'. A stifled gasp escaped his own lips as the trio locked eyes.

Erin and Veronica were transfixed like lions ready to pounce on their prey.

"Ladies?" I said with a grin, "I present you with tonight's entertainment." I held out a hand towards the shivering boy, welcoming him deeper into the room. He hesitated a moment. A moment too long for my liking. So, in a way only he could see, I glared at him and whispered, "Come in here, little one. Let them have a look at you."

Slowly and sheepishly Jaime inched forward, wobbling on the giant pink heels and his skin glowing in the vibrant lights set around the room. He positively radiated before us. And when he turned, I felt our panties collectively shift... his ass was glorious. A perfect, round, apple shaped backside split in two by his tiny, pink thong. On either side were his matching, mesh garters, and down either leg the sexy mesh mingled with the high straps of his heels. His top was nothing more than a skimpy bra with see-thru straps, showing off all manners of flesh except his nipples.

When he had creeped close enough, I motioned him towards Erin. "Jaime dear, this is Erin."

She smiled and gave a little wave. "Hi cutie. Love your outfit!"

All Jaime could do was blush.

Then I presented him to Veronica. I hadn't realized it until now but she had bathed herself in the shadows. Even her hair covered most of her face. Nevertheless I took Jaime's hand and guided him towards her. As I did she flipped her hair back and leaned forward, coming into the light.

"And this is Miss-" I began...

Her emergence stopped Jaime dead in his tracks.

"Petra!?" Jaime cut me off, his face reeling in shock.

"Oh, you know her?" I asked. Looking first to him then Veronica. How the hell did he know who she was!?

All she did was smile back at me. That sexy, sinister smile that she pulled off so well.

"She-she sometimes works at my school. S-she knows the c-coach. And some of the popular boys..." Jaime's words were a stammer of vowels.

Veronica just let out a low chuckle. "Oh?" She asked, "you know Taylor too, hmm?"

Jaime gave a weak nod.

"Aw, poor baby. Does he pick on you too?" Veronica said, hinting at far more than she was letting on.

Another nod. Jaime was beat red.

"Well don't you worry. He won't be picking on anyone else for long. Not after I'm done with him." Veronica said, grinning ear to ear.

I saw her look to Erin, their smiles unifying. A story for a different day I suppose. But for now all I wanted was to see Veronica's cock in Jaime's mouth.

"C'mere little girl..." Veronica coo'd, holding out her hands until Jaime took them. She pulled him closer, until their legs were touching and so that his navel was at her eye level. Closer now she dropped his hands so she could lean forward and run her fingers up his legs. Starting at his calves she felt him up, rising up his limbs until she gripped his plump butt with both hands.

When she squeezed I heard Jaime moan. "Mmm. Nice little ass on you," Veronica said, kneading the hunks of flesh for us to see. Hands full, she turned him so she could drag her tongue over his left ass cheek. I thought Jaime was going to faint but Veronica held him up by his fleshy backside. After another long lick she let go and leaned back into her chair.

"Why don't you dance for us, Jaime?" Veronica said, letting her hand wander over her body.

Jaime turned to me for approval. "Good idea, dear. It's okay."

Without any more hesitation, Jaime moved to the center of the room and began a slow, sultry swaying. No more than a few feet away from any of us he swiveled his hips, slowly gyrating and running his hands over his smooth, young body. He closed his eyes, running his fingertips over his chest as he moved, playing with his tits the way a female stripper would. He really was a natural.

Focusing on Veronica first, he turned around and spread his ass, displaying his bright pink, hairless hole behind his tiny, string thong.

The new angle allowed him to face Erin, and when he leaned over towards her, Jaime stuck a finger in his mouth, fellating it for Erin while he pulled his butt apart for Veronica. Finally he was playing his part and enjoying it. My eyes soaking in the sight, I could tell his tiny dick was getting hard in his pretty pink panties.

Erin slid forward in her chair, spreading her legs for the bent over boy. Her bulge was astounding, pushing on the buttons of her jean shorts so much I thought they might pop off!

Jaime bent forward, placing his hands on Erin's bare thighs to tilt even further towards her groin. Erin's hand slid behind his head, keeping him bent over at the waist. A second later and her fly was open and she had pulled her fat, slick cock from the opening. Whilst I had seen it before, these were far different circumstances. It was a beautiful piece of meat. Thicker than most but completely shaven save for a thin strip at its base.

Jaime gasped.

"You like?" Erin said.

Jaime nodded, licking his lips. He eyed the monster phallus that flexed and throbbed mere inches from his face. As he stared it flexed, growing exponentially before his eyes. And as it grew to its full eight inches, a smile crept across the boys' lips.

Then Erin gently moved his head towards the hunk of meat jutting out from her shorts, until her dickhead pressed against the boy's lips. And like the good slut that he is, Jaime instantly opened and reflexively took her whole cockhead into his waiting mouth.

"Holy shit," Erin huffed.

Jaime murmured something, engulfing her glans in an already-mouthful. Erin grunted, humming as she ran her fingers through the boy's blonde hair.

I looked over at Veronica, who was transfixed at the sight. But when she realized I was waiting on her, she smiled and stood, peeling off her top. I followed suit, pulling off my yoga pants and panties so my cock could spring forth. God it felt good to free her. I was already hard and pre-cum oozed from my tip. I couldn't wait to defile my little crossdresser slut. But movement beside me made me glance to Veronica. Down her torn pants went, a fluid, stripping motion until they hit the floor. She stepped out of them effortlessly, and that's when I saw it. She had let loose a twelve inch semi-hard monster of a girlcock that hung down to her knees.

"Holy Christ Veronica," I said in an audible gasp. I had never met anyone bigger than me! Erin came close but nothing prepared me for the sheer size of the thing she had attached to her.

Before I could act, Veronica knelt behind Jaime. She pulled his thong aside with her thumb, spread his sweet ass, and jammed her tongue inside him. Jaime squealed. Well, squealed as best he could with Erin's cock in his mouth.

I felt useless for a moment, watching my personal slut being double-ended. But with a quick smirk of realization I tore off my shirt and put a hand on Jaime's head. He still only had Erin's cockhead in his mouth, but I knew he could take more, so I had to force the issue.

"HURK!" Jaime muttered as I pushed down on the back of his skull, cramming more cock into his mouth. I nudged closer, my hard-on brushing his belly, and with my other hand pulled his butt apart for Veronica.

He moaned as I squeezed, and Veronica hungrily lapped at his hole. A trifecta of sexual groans and moans pervaded the room, Jaime, Erin and Veronica were all humming and murmuring sensual nothings as we worked.

Soon I began to slow rocking back and forth, letting the boy's body slide over the top of my shaft. His skin was so soft and his movement so forceful, just fucking the space below him was enough for me. Soon his entire naval was coated in my pre-cum and now, slick with my juices, felt amazing just sliding over it.

"Holy shit, Bree!" Erin huffed. "This little slut is amazing!"

"Tell me about it," I said, slapping Jaime on the ass. He let out a muffled moan, blushed, then dove deeper onto her rod. "How's he taste, Veronica?"

Veronica pulled her tongue out of his ass and, almost out of breath, sucked in some much needed air.

"Mmm, good enough to fuck!" She said, licking her top lip.

We giggled and I heard Jaime let out a muffled squeak when she left his asshole. But then Veronica stood, wiped her chin and smacked his plump right ass cheek. Her massive tits stood out like a shelf and her thick, veiny cock stood at almost the same ninety degree angle. "I think your little whore is ready."

After another hard SMACK on his ass, I yanked on Jaime's hair, pulling him off Erin's wet stick.

He was upright for only a moment before I directed his face to Veronica's thick cock. I saw Jaime's eyes go wide at first, staring at the monster protruding from Veronica. He let out a slight whimper but opened his mouth, sticking out his tongue so that she could plant her cockhead at his gaping, wet orifice.

"C'mon little Jaime. Open up," Veronica whispered down at him.

I could see the fear in Jaime's face as he looked at the hard, veined, monster before him.

"Go on," she coo'd, replacing my hand with hers. She tucked some of his blonde hair behind an ear and guided him onto her bulbous, purple tip. As soon as he wrapped his lips around it, she moaned, tiling her head back while still clutching his head.

"What a good boy," Veronica said, smiling down at him.

Bent over the opposite way now, Erin stood and gripped Jaime's hips. She pulled his butt apart, staring down at his tiny pink hole. I recognized the look in her eyes. The look of wonder and lust. I remember the first time I saw his little boyhole and how I couldn't wait to attack it.

Finally, after far too long of staring, Erin acted on her lust. His thong still pulled to one side, Erin lined her glistening member to the boypussy in front of her...

"Ahhh," Jaime cried, as the thick girlmeat pressed against his hole.

Veronica was quick to put his mouth back to work on her cock, her hand changing from gentle to stern in an instant.

When Erin's head 'popped' in, Jaime squealed again, letting out a girlish high-pitched cry that turned into a shuddering moan. But once again Veronica was there to silence him.

Unrelenting, Erin sank further, plunging with the aid of Veronica's saliva into Jaime's wet and waiting boypussy. Humming a guttural string of obscenities, inch by inch, Jaime's ass was filled.

But Erin wasn't one for niceties. Hell, none of us were. So in a flash she grabbed Jaime's fleshy hips and rammed the full length of her shaft all the way in!

She pushed hard, making her balls slap his panty-covered genitals.

The boy cried out again! His body twitched and convulsed but Erin and Veronica held tight. Holding his nubile body in place for their fulfillment. They, like me, were not done yet. Far from it.

Veronica wasted no time, thrusting her hips in a vicious fervor. She began to fuck his mouth, taking advantage of his throat each time he tried to yelp. As she pumped, grabbing Jaime's head of blonde hair, Erin slowly fucked the young teen's hole on the opposite end. I was astounded! Erin was nearly buried in the boy and Veronica had nearly half her cock in his throat. It must have been the angle, still bent over ninety degrees, that allowed such a seamless fucking.

While I slammed Jaime's head down onto more and more of her shaft, Veronica reached down and un-fastened Jaime's bra, letting his tiny breasts free. When the garment fell she moved both hands to his hair, making a ponytail with her grip so she could thrust harder and faster.

Jaime moaned louder while he was spit roasted, soon pushing his ass back on Erin and opening his jaw for Veronica.

I stood there, my mouth dry, my own fat cock hard as nails as I took in the scene. Never had I seen anything so hot in my life. Watching two mammoth girlcocks sliding in and out of Jaime's holes made my own womanhood leak pre-cum beyond words. I knew there would be many, many more times in the future where I would whore out young Jaime. Just knowing I owned this kid, and he would have to take any cock I told him to, made my heart pound.

With one final thrust, Erin screamed, plunging her dick to its base. Her balls contracted. Her leg twitched. Jaime moaned again, allowing Veronica to cram the entire length down his esophagus. Her heavy balls hit his chin. Jaime's eyes rolled back into his head. From behind, Erin gripped the boy tight ready to unload!

"FUUUCK!" Erin grunted, gripping Jaime's reddened ass with both hands as she emptied herself into his guts. As she finished, Veronica unsheathed herself, letting Jaime finally breathe.

Despite his deep gasps, Jaime whimpered as both cocks left him. Then holding himself up, fucked Erin still, grinding onto her softening meat. I could hardly believe it! He was milking Erin's cock despite having just been brutally throatfucked.

But before he could milk the last drop, the duo collectively spun Jaime around. He was thrown off balance for a moment, before Veronica gripped his hips and spread his legs. Erin, grabbing Jaime by his hair, pulled his face to her groin.

"Time to clean up the mess!" She huffed, nearly out of breath. Jaime opened his mouth, letting his tongue fall out, and Erin dragged him up and over her slimy cock.

On the other end of Jaime's body, Veronica prepared him. She spread his legs, placed a hand on his back, and sat her girth between his fleshy butt cheeks. He moaned as she started gyrating, moving her meat between his ass, fucking his meaty buttocks. Yet his moans were mixed with whimpers as he no doubt realized, or felt, how big the next cock was. Her womanhood was massive. It had to be at least twelve inches long and almost as fat as a beer can.

I could see Jaime physically shake as Veronica grabbed him by the arms and bent him over.

Biting her lip, Veronica placed her throbbing head against Jaime's wet exit. She spread his legs further apart, getting one more look at his just-fucked hole before placing her wet cockhead at the opening. Then, with one hard push, the fat head popped into the slut's pussy!

"OH-" Jaime cried out! But Veronica didn't give him a moment to adjust. She just slammed her throbbing weapon into him, cramming nearly half of it inside! "Oh God!" Jaime screamed. "It wont fit! It's not gonna fit!"

But I don't think any words could stop her. Instead she just started pounding the boy, pinning his arms behind his back. Erin silenced his cries with meat of her own, forcing him to lap at her balls, literally using his mouth as she wished. Jaime screamed into the gag and tears flowed from his eyes as his anal tract was stretched like never before. Veronica was ruthless, hammering as fast and as hard as she could. She was getting deeper with each thrust, and soon she was fully buried in the boy's hot, young ass.

Jaime moaned and groaned between them, his panties now wet from cum of his own.

I was having a hard time controlling myself as Veronica feverishly fucked his cum filled hole. Just knowing that Erin had just fucked him, that another 'woman' had just used him and that even now Veronica's cock was pushing cum deeper into my boy's fuckhole, sent me over the edge. I had barely touched myself but I was about to cum just from watching. Not wanting to waste anything, I stepped beside Erin, grabbed Jaime by the hair, and jammed my dick into his mouth. Erin's semi still inside, I shot my load instantly, mixing our cum inside my slut's sweet little mouth.

"Mmm, fuck!" I huffed, letting ounce after ounce fill Jaime's pipes and dribble out of his mouth. He swallowed what he could, I could tell, but being violently fucked from behind would make anything difficult. Even after my balls had emptied he kept fellating me, licking up what cum spilled onto myself or his chin.

Yet even when the cleaning was done, when Erin and I's cocks went soft and fell out of Jaime's mouth, Veronica was still pulverizing him. I had heard stories of her sexual stamina but this was insanity. Standing for a better look, I watched her entire piping hot length careening in and out of the boy's ass, jack hammering like a piston. With no penis to quiet his cries, his painful screams quickly returned, rattling off the house's walls and into the night.

"P-P-PLEASE! G-G-GOD!" Jaime screamed. "M-M-MY A-A-ASS! I-I-IT H-H-HURTS"

As much as I loved hearing him beg, I didn't want my neighbors to think I was murdering someone. So thinking quick, I snatched up my pair of panties off the floor, still drenched in my pre-cum and shoved it into Jaime's mouth.

Then kneeling, I clutched Jaime's face, holding it close to mine, and whispered, "I told you boy." I had to almost shout to hear myself over the wet sloshing and slapping bouncing around the room. "You're gonna learn your place, bitch! You're nothing more than a pathetic little faggot! A whore we'll use at will. I fuckin' own you, slut! And you'll do whatever I want. Whatever WE want! You're nothing more than a girly fuck-hole!"

I stood up and smiled at Veronica as she still pummeled away. Her hair was a mess and she was covered in sweat, giving her stunning body a sexy, olive shine. She smiled back and slapped Jaime's ass, cramming her insanely huge cock into the young high schooler. Her breathing heightened. I could tell she was getting close. But she didn't slow down. Not in the slightest.

Jaime's yelps stuttered into the gag as Veronica slowed finally, pulling her cock all the way out of the boy to admire the gaping hole, before driving it base-deep again. It was almost inhuman: she'd pull out, her fat gleaming shaft exiting like an anaconda slithering out of its den, only to rechamber the tip of her cock against the ravaged boypussy so she could ram it all the way back in! Jaime wailed into the gag each time she re-entered him with those long, hard strokes. Erin and I merely enjoyed the show as the busty amazonian beauty mercilessly emasculated the sissy boy. Before long we were both hard again, and we slowly began stroking our girlcock's. To my surprise, Erin smiled at me then reached over, gently gripping my hard-on while she played with her own.

Suddenly, Veronica pulled her cock out of Jaime's ass with a wet 'pop'!

Erin and I both snapped to attention!

The poor boy may have well been made of jelly! Without Veronica holding him up, his legs went out and he collapsed to the floor. She was on him in an instant, following him down to her knees. Quickly and roughly, Veronica knelt and flipped him over onto his back. Then grabbing either of his ankles, she spread them apart, aligned her cock to his asshole and shoved her meat back in.

"MMRRPH!" Jaime cried, my panties still stuffed down his windpipe.

Erin looked at me and smiled, swiftly diving to the floor by Jaime's upper half. I followed suit, kneeling so our hardening dicks stretched out over his neck and face. His arms free he reached out, grabbing for our shafts so he could immediately start jacking them. I couldn't believe it! My little slut wanted more!

I pulled out Jaime's gag, and he just moaned and blabbered gibberish, craning his neck towards Erin and I's dicks. We knelt closer on either side of him, reaching over to tweak either respective nipple. Jaime let loose a fresh round of loud moans, tonguing the air until he was finally able to reach my cockhead. His mouth felt so good, and he jerked Erin off while he sucked me. I kept on working his nipples, watching his pathetic little prick twitch inside his panties with each twist. It was so small, it didn't even poke out of his waistband. They were soaked through, and soon I saw why. Each time Veronica drove her length into him, a new spurt of cum would saturate the fabric and he convulsed in a loud, vocal orgasm! There was no telling how many times he had come, literally drenching and filling his panties with teenage sperm - all without touching his little dick once!

What a good boy.

Leaning over him, I cupped his face, fucking his mouth. Erin was opposite me, Jaime's free left hand feverishly jacking her cock. The scene was too hot. His mouth was too good. In just a tense few minutes I was ready to cum again. I didn't want it to end but his lips and mouth were just too amazing.

"Almost there little slut, keep sucking for mommy's seed!" I said, cupping my breasts.

Erin was close too. She fucked his hand while he jerked her off, but then Jaime switched cocks, sucking her instead while he jerked me.

Back and forth he rotated, slobbering on both our meat poles. When Veronica's hammering had reached its peak and I could feel her orgasm stirring, I leaned down, mashing my tits against Jaime's collarbone. While he was still being violently fucked, I whispered to him again, "you like this, slut? You like being used by our big cocks?"

As he came down from his latest orgasmic high, huffed, "Y-Y-yes Miss B-Becker! P-Please..." He panted. Veronica dropped one leg so she could wrap her arms around the other, hammering him sideways now. He traded Erin's dick for mine, licking over its helmet before taking it back in his mouth.

"Please what?" I said, my balls swelling.

When he switched back to Erin's piece he slathered more words, "M-More! I want it!"

"Mmm, good girl." I hummed. And then I felt his lips back on me. His tongue did its job and I buckled, sending a stream of hot cum into his mouth! He couldn't take it all though and it spilt out across his face.

Then Erin yelped! Jaime tried to turn to catch her load but failed.

Like two broken spigots our cocks fired, sending white ropes of semen across his face, neck and chest. A second later and he was moaning like before. Now it was Veronica's turn...

Pinning his leg against his body, Veronica pressed down onto him. Her breasts engulfed his calf and her body trapped his smooth, pale leg against his chest so she could hammer him into the floor! With her new angle, she dragged her tongue from his belly button to his chin, lapping up the trails of semen. When her face rose next to his she spit our cum into his mouth, fucking him non-stop.

"Beg for it, bitch!" Veronica huffed! "Tell me what you are!"

There was a brief beat. Jaime's brain had to come to its senses. But as Veronica tensed up for her orgasm, he moaned and screamed!

"Miss Petra... I'm a slut. I'm a cock hungry whore." Veronica's pace picked up. Her balls slapped against his flesh harder and HARDER! "Fuck my little pussy! Use me! I need your cum inside me! My only purpose is to be used. Please cum in me! That's what I'm for! God I'm such a little faggot! Use my fucking hole!"

And Veronica obliged. She was like an animal, grunting and fucking. Her entire length sliding in and out, in and out!

"Oh God, oh God, oh God! Fuck me! FUCK ME, MISS PETRA! OH GOD, PLEASE! PLEASE CUM IN ME!!!"

As Jaime verbalized what he truly was, he shot another load into his already wet panties.

Then finally, Veronica buried her entire length of pipe into the teenage hole and SCREAMED, letting out a primal yell as she unfurled a pint of hot girlcum deep into Jaime's guts!

Jaime cried out with her, his face streaked in mascara and eyeliner. His eyes rolled white! His body spasmed. He clutched Veronica tight as wave after wave of sexual intensity washed over him.

She didn't pull out. Instead she held him there. On her thick cock. Veins popping over her arms and legs, she pushed a gust of air out of her lungs, cumming hard. She knelt there, legs tucked under her, her cock pumping and throbbing, figuratively impregnating young Jaime for what seemed like an hour.

The next thing I knew Jaime was shuddering one final time. I looked and noticed, watching Veronica slowly pulling her foot long cock from Jaime's rectum. His convulsions were almost involuntary. And when she finally unsheathed her spear, he crumpled and shivered briefly before passing out completely.

Exhausted and satisfied, we all collapsed on top of Jaime. Covered in sweat and cum, we each looked at one another with a smile. My slut had lived up to his reputation. With Veronica and Erin now in on the fun, it was going to be one hell of a weekend...

THE END (of Part Three)

BONUS CHAPTER: MY EPILOGUE

The next few weeks were pretty much the same. I was fucking Jaime multiple times a day, seven times a week. After he quit his job at the complex as the resident 'pool boy' I convinced his mother to have him come and 'work' for me as a housekeeper. She was dubious at first, but I put on my best proud-confident-businesswoman-act and she fell for it. Doubly so because Jaime practically begged her for the job.

Afterwards, calling my little boywhore or having him come visit was standard fare. I would even pick him up at school on Fridays and take him back to the spa. Sometimes, we would close up early on those afternoons, the perks of practically owning the place. There, Erin and I would fuck the boy for hours, leaving gallons of cum inside his sweet, young, eager body.

Sometimes we would take turns, other times we'd ravage him simultaneously. Regardless, Jaime always returned home with an ass and belly full of cum.

The first time I brought Jaime back to the spa was a day to remember! It started as an impromptu 'yoga' session, but after everyone had left for the day, we used the teen slut until the sun went down.

Assuming dominant, 'instructor' roles, Erin and I bent and folded my little Jaime in all sorts of lewd positions, all the while brushing our bodies against his. After he became flustered we made him worship us, massaging our sweaty bodies until we were rock hard. Afterwards, we made him strip us nude and grovel at our feet until he begged us to use him.

And use him we did.

We fucked my little boywhore rough that night, stuffing girlcock, balls deep, down either hole. Erin chose his throat, quickly stuffing her length down his windpipe, cutting off his air supply until he was panicking and struggling. I plundered his ass, slamming him repeatedly with no regard for his whimpering cries. Our wet bodies made heavy slapping sounds as we railed him, sending sweat splattering against the floor mats.

Finally, Erin pulled out, letting Jaime gasp for air before slamming herself back down his throat. I came inside him, as he choked on Erin's cock. It felt so good when his body convulsed and that slick boypussy squeezed extra tight. After dumping my load in his greedy hole, Erin pulled her cock out of Jaime's throat and painted his face with cum as the boy gasped for air.

We left him there that night, a glorious canvas of semen. The girls' who opened in the morning nearly called the police when they found him, but I arrived just in time to whisk him away. The rest of the weekend was business as usual.

Anytime we were at my apartment, Jaime had a 'uniform' that he was always required to wear. Although 'uniform' implies a fair bit of clothing, it was basically just a collar, stockings, heels and a chastity cage. I know I mentioned I was never one for crossdressing, but after Jaime showed such a affliction to the wares, I couldn't resist letting him degrade himself!

Onward, like our first weekend together, it became commonplace to use Jaime whenever, and wherever I wanted.

Sometimes I would take him to the gym with me, usually in some sort of feminine, sissy attire. My latest ensemble for him was a tiny white sports bra and a pair of matching running shorts. They were skin tight, and the bottom of his ass cheeks stuck out the bottom, leaving little to anyone's imagination. The sheerness also ensured his tiny genitals or cage clearly showed through the fabric.

He looked like a true slut, but I didn't care, and reveled in how embarrassed my little whore was by it. Besides, holy shit did he get some looks!

Men and women alike, some in shock and others with interest.

One night, there was an attractive young man at the gym with us, brimming with muscle, pumping away at a few hundred pounds of steel, who just couldn't seem to take his eyes off my little Jaime. I had seen the stud before, and never took him for gay, not with such an amazing body, but after a quick chat, it was all but confirmed.

He told me his name was Brad, and played football at the local college. I thought about taking him for myself but thought it may be challenging since he was a top. Instead, after a short conversation, Brad headed into the men's locker room and I strutted back to where Jaime was sitting.

"What did you do?" My cute little toy asked.

"You just made me fifty bucks," I said cheerfully.

"Huh?"

I chuckled, "wait another minute, then head into the locker room. That young man that was working out over there would like to meet you."

"What?" Jaime quipped. "Did you just... pimp me out?"

I responded sharply. "How many times do I have to tell you, Jaime?! Don't question me. You're mine to use as I see fit, and you're going to suck some cock if I say so!"

Jaime shrank, eyeballing the door to the locker room like it was the entrance to a haunted house.

I have to admit, my cock started to get hard thinking about him and the anonymous stud.

"Times up," I said to him, tapping my wrist as if I was wearing a watch.

Without saying a word, Jaime rose and slowly crept into the next room while I finished my last few reps. Astonishingly, just a few minutes later, my boywhore returned, face red, nipples poking through his top, and his top soaked through with saliva.

"Well?" I asked, slapping the bar down on the bench press.

"It's done. He wants to meet me here again next week."

I smiled, "we'll see. Get your stuff, let's go."

My cock was hard as a rock all the way home. The second we stepped into my apartment, I grabbed Jaime and threw him face down on the floor. Ass in the air, I could clearly make out his worn hole through his practically see-thru shorts. I tore them apart with my bare hands and felt his cunt. It was nice and wet.

He must have fingered himself while he sucked that guy off.

I pulled down the front of my workout shorts, letting my fat cock and plump balls pop free, and lined up my throbbing cockhead to Jaime's hole. Pushing hastily, I slid myself in, grunting as I felt the warm wetness envelop my cock.

"Tell me about it whore," I demanded. "Tell me about that stud's cock. Tell me what it was like to be sold."

"Ahh," Jaime wailed. "Wasn't as big as yours. He had me suck it until it got hard, then he pushed me against the wall, held my head, and fucked my throat!"

Moans took hold of his vocal chords as I pummeled him.

"Keep going!" I huffed. "What else?!"

"Mmph! Mmph! W-we could hear the other people in the locker room. He didn't care. My head kept hitting the tile but he just kept going! When he came he held me down, came down in my tummy! I was so embarrassed! We could hear a man in the shower next to us as he filled me up!"

After hearing his slutty tale I couldn't hold back anymore, and groaned as I gave Jaime a fresh batch of my virile seed. He took it all, and I envisioned my cum meeting with Brad's somewhere in Jaime's intestines, mingling within and solidifying my slut's whorishness.

Afterwards, still snickering from the all-new-level of degradation, I left my blown out fuckdoll lying on the carpet, panting and trembling. It truly was a night to remember.

The following day just so happened to be another Friday, and Jaime's mother was going out of town. So we went to his house for a change, planning on spending the weekend there.

Little did I know it would change things forever.

Walking into the quaint little home was something akin to a dream. His mother, Alice, decorated everything like some model home in a sitcom, with flowers and brightly colored furniture in every room. I remember standing in the entryway, watching as Jaime strutted in, moving his hands as he informed me of the various portions of the house.

"Where's your room?" I asked, interrupting him.

"Up…upstairs," he replied meekly.

"Show me."

We traveled there, and when we entered, Jaime crawled up on his bed, placed his cheek against a pillow, and pulled down his tight jeans to expose his luscious ass.

Bottomless and waiting, ass in the air, he looked at me over one shoulder. Such a good slut.

I swung the duffel bag I had brought over my shoulder, letting it hit the floor with a loud, convoluted 'thudding' sound, then unzipped it.

"I've got a surprise for you," I said, pulling the gigantic black dildo from within.

Jaime's mouth dropped open and his eyes grew wide at the sight of it. The dildo was an impressive fourteen inches and thick as a wrist. I told him we were going to make it fit.

"Actually, two surprises." I said as I pulled my phone from my back pocket, watching the concern grow on his face.

In a flash I had the camera pointing at his delicious, upturned bottom. I sat it across from us, making sure it was propped up in such a way that it could see the room in full. Then I made my way towards him, giving Jaime's ass a squeeze. I could feel his body flush just at my touch, but he moaned when I slid the dildo between his creamy, bulbous buns.

I fucked the cleft of his ass for a few moments, letting occasional spindles of saliva drip off my bottom lip and down onto the plastic tool. When the large, black appendage was sufficiently wet, I placed the fat pink head against his tiny, winking hole.

"OOooOOoo," Jaime trembled.

I closed my eyes and relished in his battered hole trying to wrap around my cock.

"Yesssss!" I hissed.

"Mom-mommy! Mmmooommmyyy!"

"Yes baby, take mommy's cock!" My eyes were still closed. My head was still rolling. I had no idea that he was actually looking back behind us.

"Nnnooo! Miss-Miss Becker! Mommy!"

My orgasm knocked me from my dream-like rutting. I howled as we both came in unison. My cock exploded inside him, sending semen sputtering out the sides and onto the bed.

That's when I saw Jaime's eyes, looking back towards the door, and the look of absolute terror on his face...

"What in heaven's name is going on here?!" A voice cried out behind me.

I remember thinking: What the fuck!? Having just cum, words and thought wasn't quite working yet. I turned, twisted really, back towards the bedroom door, and locked eyes with Jaime's mother, who looked on in utter shock.

"Alice!?" I blurted, inadvertently pulling myself and the dildo out of my personal little cocksleeve. Jaime's asshole pulsed as it opened wider and a river of cum poured out.

"Bri-Brianna!?" She stuttered, "What are you? How? You have a-"

I watched, still in some shock, as she tried to speak, and noticed how wide her eyes got as they traveled down my body, fixating on my wet, semi-hard cock. Alice was a beautiful woman, and a young mother. She had long blonde hair, narrow shoulders, and an ample bust. It was clear where Jaime got such lovely genes.

Her eyes strayed far longer than I expected, even after I turned completely around to face her. My slippery, throbbing womanhood swung around with me, slinging cum across the carpet in a half-circle.

"A cock? Why yes, I do!" I smiled as I moved, "secrets out now I guess. You can see why Jaime frickin' loves me so much."

My words shook her gaze off my gleaming genitals and back to her effeminate son, ass still in the air, lying face down on the bed. I glanced back too, smiling at his blown out hole still leaking cum. Jaime himself wheezed and panted, cross-eyed, unable to move.

When I turned back around I was standing in front of Alice, the petite but voluptuous woman cowering below me. She wasn't much taller than Jaime, so I had about a foot on her, putting her eye level with my big, hefty tits.

"I… don't know what to say…" She muttered, cheeks turning a rosy red.

I smiled and said, "You don't have to say anything. You just have to clean my cock."

I didn't really think she would do it. In fact I was sure she'd spout some religious nonsense and try to kick me out of her house. But instead, giving me a lovely view of her cleavage as she knelt, Alice got to her knees.

"I've seen the way you look at me," I whispered back, causing Alice's gaze to shift from my meaty appendage. "You think it's disgusting, don't you?"

"N-no! I…" She shook her head rapidly, still unable to look away.

"Maybe you should prove it?" I continued, placing both hands on my hips. I cocked my hips, making my cock wiggle.

With a gulp, Alice put her face level with my crotch.

"It... smells funny..." She grimaced.

"Course it does. It was just up your little teenage whore's ass."

Despite scrunching her nose, the woman leaned forward. Funny, her words said one thing, but her body said something else entirely.

"Thaaat's it," I said in a mocking tone. "Let's see if you suck cock as good as your son."

She reached out with both hands, slowly placing them on either of my thighs. Little by little, she inched toward the thick, veiny cock-meat that twitched and throbbed back to life before her eyes.

She ran her gaze across my vein-ridden womanhood, trying no doubt to estimate its length.

"I know you're getting turned on, Alice, but I'm getting impatient," I said, glaring down. "Less staring, more sucking."

"I-I am not getting turned on!" she protested, averting her eyes after an embarrassingly long time of inspecting my genitals. It was immensely satisfying, looking down at her red cheeks. The cross on her necklace that was nestled in her cleavage rising and falling between her heaving chest.

After a deep breath, she continued, "It's just that... I've never seen one so big..."

I could literally hear her heart pounding as she grabbed the middle of my shaft. She closed her eyes just as her luscious lips came into contact with my thick glans, giving it a slow, overly sensual kiss.

"Oh no, keep your eyes open, Alice," I instructed, tucking some strands of hair behind her ear. "I want you to look. Worship it."

Her facial expression remained the same as before, timid and submissive. With eyes open, she resumed, planting another kiss on the tip, then another few ones along my length, all the way down my underside.

Hesitatingly, Alice parted her lips and let her tongue slip out, giving a long, wet lick against the bottom of my smooth, warm shaft. Just like she had worked down while kissing it, she licked again and again while moving her mouth back to the tip, where it all culminated in a long, drawn out slather with her whole tongue against my precum-leaking slit, taking in the sticky fluid into her mouth and swallowing reluctantly.

"Keep going," I commanded, "Let's see if you have what it takes to suck a better cock than your sissy son."

Her entire face flushed a deep red, and her eyes seductively half-closed, fluttering occasionally when she nearly gagged on my inflamed tip.

She was actually kind of pretty like that. Afterall, Alice was a beautiful woman. But with my fat cocktip in her mouth, and her puffy pink lips wrapped around it, she was positively amazing.

"You're pretty good at this, Alice..." I purred, running my hand through her hair. "But your tongue isn't gonna be enough. Let me see how much you can take, baby."

She moved her focus to the tip of my cock, turning and twisting her head so she could suckle on my mouth-filling glans. She had to open up quite wide to let the phallic intruder in all the way, but once she did, she closed her lips tightly around the shaft, just past the rim of the head.

"Mm... Yes, baby, just like that..." I hissed from above.

The woman kicked it up a notch, grabbing my cock with both hands, one around the base and one around the middle of my shaft, using them to jerk me off while her lips and tongue suckling my tip like it was the last lollipop on Earth.

"Damn..." I swooned, legs trembling from pleasure. "Looks like sucking cock is a skill that runs in the family..."

Alice glanced up, giving me a look that walked a line between embarrassment and anger.

"Oh fuck, Alice..." I gasped, biting my lip and taking a deep breath. "You're gonna make me... Oh, shit..."

Grabbing the lush head of blonde hair, I let out a loud moan that could almost be classified as a delirious scream. My veiny shaft throbbed hard and erupted with cum, filling the young mother's mouth in an instant. There was so much the woman had to break away, spewing cum as she did, retching onto her tits.

The next rope shot out in an arc that painted a line across Alice's face, chin to hairline. The next bursts struck her lips, nose and eyelids, quickly making her pretty features indistinguishable under a thick layer of white, gooey girl-cum. My long-winded orgasm continued, holding on to give young Alice a complete facial.

Time seemed to slow, and before long it looked like someone had dumped a bucket of white paint on her.

"God fucking damn, Alice..." I panted, admiring my handiwork with a lick of my lips. "What a nasty girl you turned out to be."

Like wearing a second skin Alice sat there on her knees, coated in my cum. It hung off her chin in thick, sticky strings that were slowly dripping off, collecting in the mix amidst her cleavage.

"Did I..." Alice began, speaking up at me blindly. Her v-cut shirt was utterly soaked, and her tits glimmered with saliva and semen. "Did I do good?"

I snickered, "I think I need to try your other holes to be sure."

She smiled from beneath the thick blanket of cum.

And just like that, I knew I had made a new fucktoy. Mother and 'son'.

Told you that day changed everything.

THE END (For real this time)

ABOUT THE AUTHOR

Jordan Bailey

Jordan Bailey is a transwoman originally from England who now lives quietly in the United States. Her hobbies include writing, movies and playing with her dogs. Lover of anime, manga and animals, she primarily writes about Futanari, or 'Dickgirl' women  and crossdressing. She also enjoys weaving tales about effeminate young men, a.k.a. 'femboys', transwomen and other transgender themes!

To get updates, send feedback, or anything else, follow her on Twitter @tehjordanbailey

www.ingramcontent.com/pod-product-compliance
Lightning Source LLC
Chambersburg PA
CBHW052142220626
47052CB00005B/1168